ADAPTED BY

Teresa Mlawer

ILLUSTRATED BY

Olga Cuéllar

Jack and the Beanstalk

Adirondack Books

Once upon a time there was a widow who lived with her only son in a small cabin in a forest. Jack and his mother were very poor; they had lost the little they had to a giant who stole from all the neighbors in the village. The only thing they had left was a cow that gave them enough milk and cheese to survive.

One day, their old cow could not give any more milk. Jack's mother asked him to take the cow to the market to see if he could sell her. Jack tied a rope around the cow's neck and happily went to town.

Along the way he met a rancher.

"Where are you going with that cow?" asked the rancher.

"I'm going to the market to sell her," replied Jack.

Upon hearing this, the rancher pulled out five beans from his pocket and said:

"These are magical beans. If you plant them, by the next morning, they will have grown into a beanstalk as tall as the sky. I'll trade the beans for your cow."

Jack thought it was a good deal, so he gave the rancher the cow in exchange for the beans, and happily hurried back home.

When his mother saw what he had done, she
was so upset that she threw the beans out of
the window and started crying inconsolably.
That night, Jack went to bed without supper.

But when Jack woke up in the morning, he was surprised to see that the beans had sprouted and a huge stalk, with many branches, reached up into the sky. Full of curiosity, he started climbing the stalk, reaching higher and higher,

until he arrived at a beautiful place with a marvelous castle. He peeked through a window and saw a giant and his wife seated at a table, ordering a hen to lay a golden egg.

Since he was very hungry, Jack knocked on the door and asked the giant's wife for something to eat. The wife, who had a good heart, told him to come in and hide until her husband took a nap. As soon as the giant fell asleep, she gave Jack a glass of milk and some cookies.

He had hardly finished eating when the giant woke up
very agitated and said:

Fee, Fie, Fo, Fum.

I smell a child's meat.

A child I'd like to eat.

Dinner will be luscious...

From hair to bones, delicious!

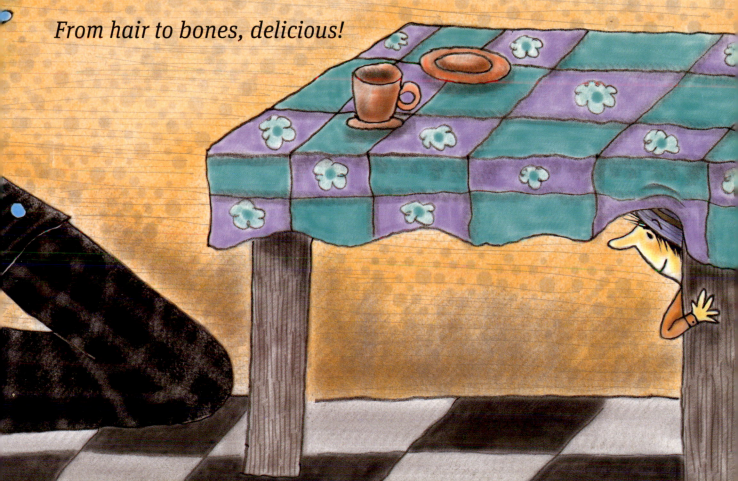

Frightened by the giant, Jack grabbed the hen and put her in a bag. He jumped out the window and quickly climbed down the stalk until he reached the ground.

His Mother was very happy when she saw the hen that laid golden eggs.

Now they could sell the eggs to buy food.

Time went by, and one day, the hen stopped laying eggs. Once again, Jack climbed the beanstalk to the castle to search for other riches they could sell for food.

This time, as Jack peeked through the window, he saw the giant counting gold coins from a big leather sack.

Once again, Jack entered the castle with the help of the giant's wife. As soon as the giant fell asleep, Jack snatched the sack of coins and quickly made his way down the stalk until he reached his house.

Now he and his mother would have enough money to live for the rest of their lives.

However, Jack could not stop thinking about the castle, with the treasures and adventures hidden behind its doors. So he decided to climb the stalk and visit it one last time.

When he approached the window, he saw that the giant was taking a nap, and next to him was a golden harp that was playing a beautiful melody without anyone touching the strings. Jack decided to go in and hide, but soon fell asleep to the sound of such beautiful music.

Suddenly, the giant woke up and started screaming:

"Wife, tell me, where have you hidden that child now?"

"What child are you talking about? There is no child here."

Furious, he shouted again:

Fee, Fie, Fo, Fum.

I smell a child's meat.

A child I'd like to eat.

Dinner will be luscious...

From hair to bones, delicious!

While the giant and his wife were arguing, Jack grabbed the harp, jumped out the window, and rapidly began climbing down the stalk.

But this time, to his surprise, he saw that the giant was following him very closely.

When Jack was close to the ground, he called out to his mother:
"Mother, hurry and bring me an axe! The giant is coming after me."
As soon as Jack reached the ground, he took the axe, and with
one hard blow cut down the beanstalk. The mean giant crashed
to the ground.

Jack and his mother shared the gold coins with their neighbors; from that day on they all lived happily, and in harmony.

TEXT COPYRIGHT ©2014 BY TERESA MLAWER / ILLUSTRATION COPYRIGHT©2014 BY ADIRONDACK BOOKS

ALL RIGHTS RESERVED. NO PART OF THIS BOOK MAY BE REPRODUCED OR TRANSMITTED IN ANY FORM OR BY ANY MEANS, ELECTRONIC OR MECHANICAL, INCLUDING PHOTOCOPYING, RECORDING OR BY ANY INFORMATION STORAGE AND RETRIEVAL SYSTEM, WITHOUT PERMISSION FROM THE PUBLISHER.

FOR INFORMATION, PLEASE CONTACT ADIRONDACK BOOKS, P.O. BOX 266, CANANDAIGUA, NEW YORK 14424.

ISBN 978-0-9883253-9-5   10 9 8 7 6 5 4 3 2   PRINTED IN CHINA